Grandfather's Key

Written by
Amanda Dauvin
Illustrated by
Floyd Yamyamin

Grandfather's Key

Tellwell Talent
www.tellwell.ca

ISBN
978-0-2288-2957-7 (Hardcover)
978-0-2288-2955-3 (Paperback)
978-0-2288-2956-0 (eBook)

- For Marc, Ella, Oliver, Rocky, & Tandy -
My Heart, my Keys, and my Furbabies.

Eva waved goodbye to her mom as she closed the front door behind her.

Every Saturday, Eva visited her grandfather, who lived at the end of the block, for breakfast. However, this Saturday was extra special.

This Saturday was Eva's birthday and she was turning seven.

Eva was very excited to be seven years old. It meant she was allowed to walk to her grandfather's house all by herself, and she could also stay up later on weekends. She wondered what other new and exciting things seven would bring.

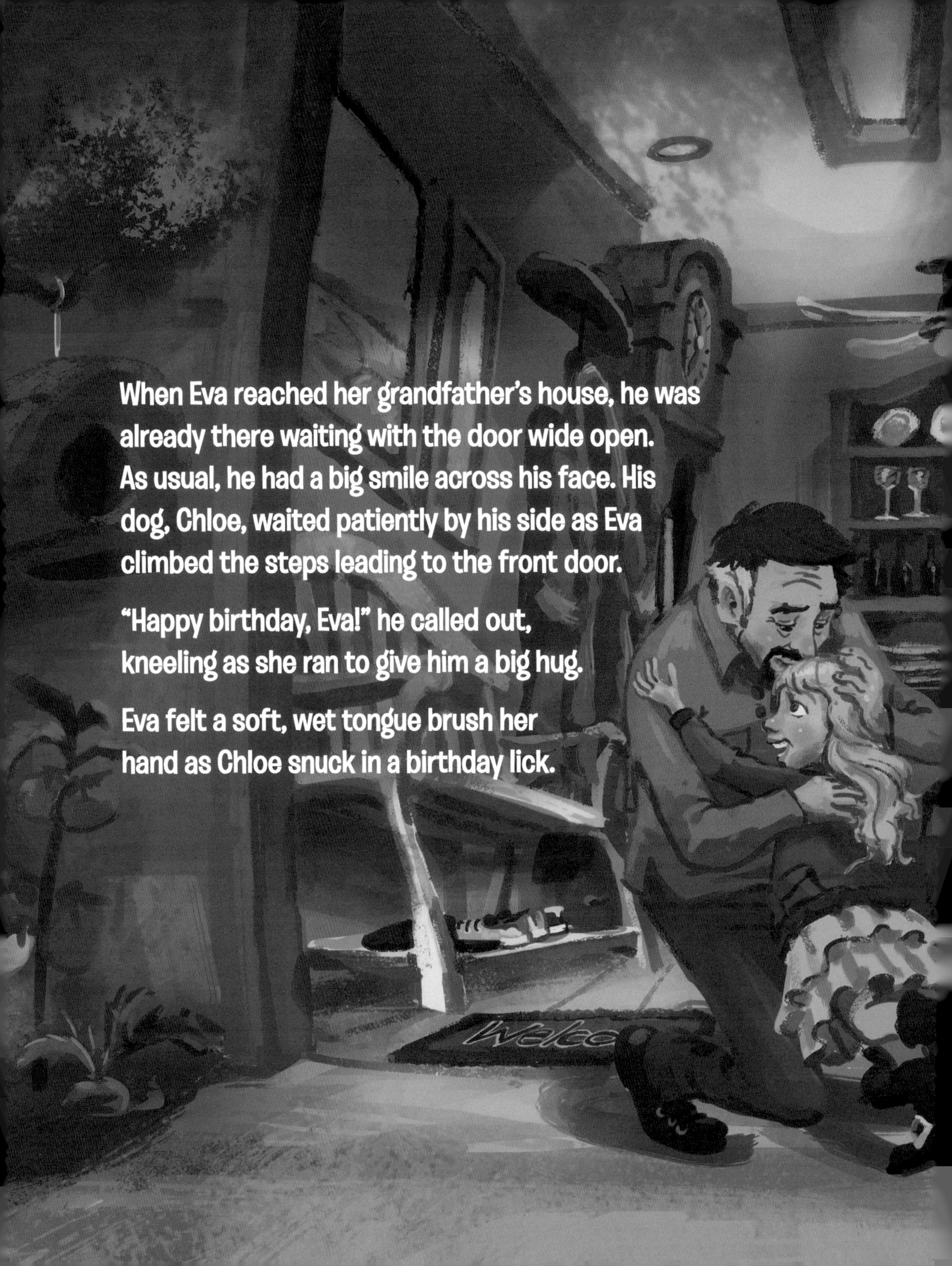

When Eva reached her grandfather's house, he was already there waiting with the door wide open. As usual, he had a big smile across his face. His dog, Chloe, waited patiently by his side as Eva climbed the steps leading to the front door.

"Happy birthday, Eva!" he called out, kneeling as she ran to give him a big hug.

Eva felt a soft, wet tongue brush her hand as Chloe snuck in a birthday lick.

“Now let’s see,” her grandfather said playfully. “You must be ten.”

“No, Grandfather,” Eva laughed, knowing he was teasing her.

“Four?” he asked, winking.

“I’m seven, Grandfather!” Eva said, giggling.

“Wow, seven!” he said, eyes twinkling. “Well, I know exactly what seven-year-olds like for their birthday breakfast, Eva. Blueberry pancakes!”

Eva was not a picky eater. In fact, she liked most foods. But blueberry pancakes were her absolute favorite, and she couldn’t wait for her grandfather’s special birthday breakfast.

Once inside, Eva took off her coat, which she hung neatly on a hook by the door.

When she bent down to remove her shoes, she saw a little box wrapped in lovely purple paper with a pink bow and a tag that had her name on it.

"Is this for me?" Eva asked.

"It sure is," her grandfather replied, rubbing his hands together in eager anticipation. "Would you like to open it now?"

"Yes please," Eva said, delighted. She loved opening presents.

Eva removed the pretty purple paper and inside there was a shiny blue box with white polka dots. She opened the little box and found a small golden key on a delicate chain. It was beautiful.

“Do you like it?” her grandfather asked, taking the necklace out of the box and fastening it around her neck.

“I love it, Grandfather. Thank you!” she said, giving him a warm hug. “But what does this key open?”

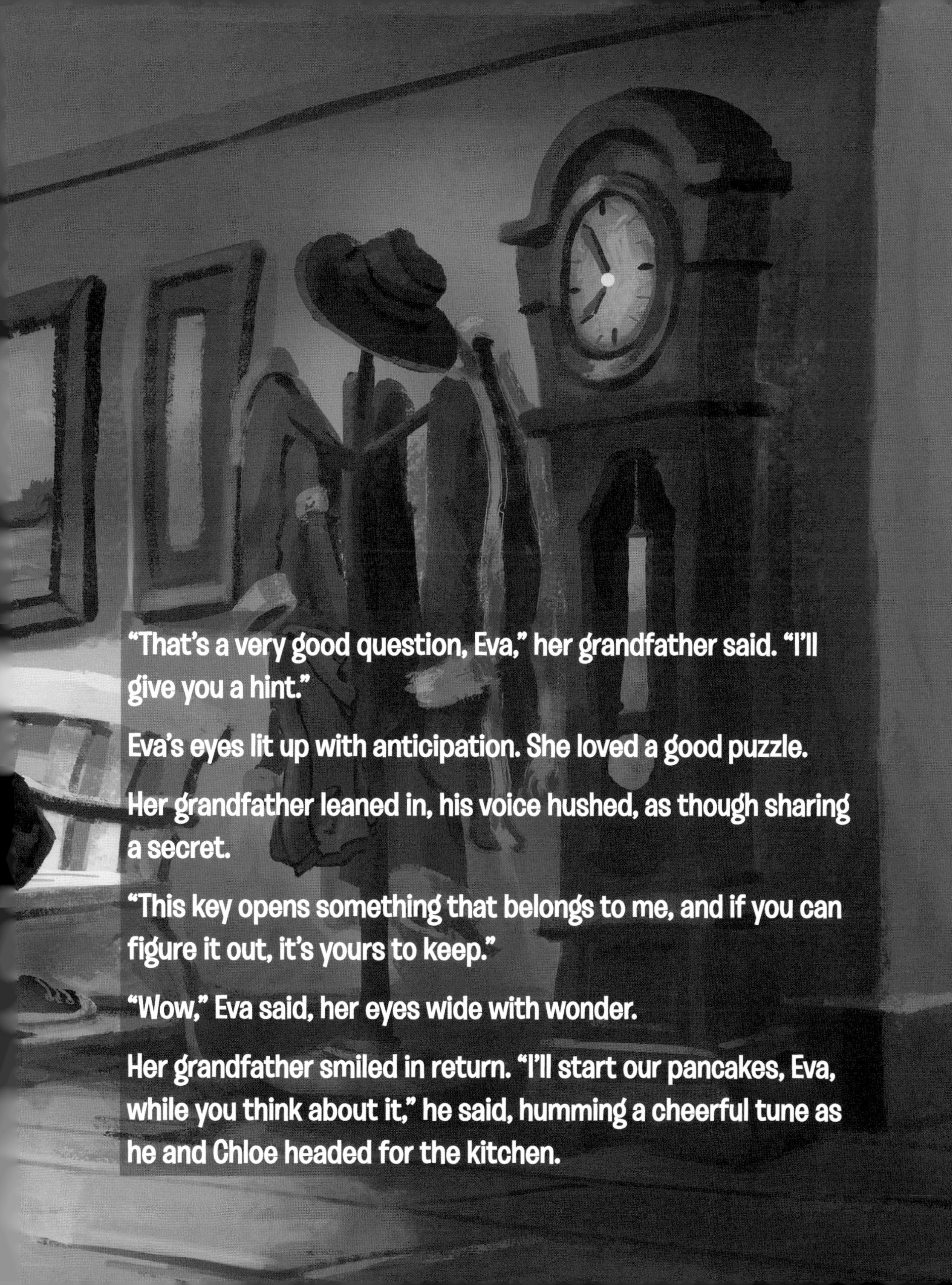

“That’s a very good question, Eva,” her grandfather said. “I’ll give you a hint.”

Eva’s eyes lit up with anticipation. She loved a good puzzle.

Her grandfather leaned in, his voice hushed, as though sharing a secret.

“This key opens something that belongs to me, and if you can figure it out, it’s yours to keep.”

“Wow,” Eva said, her eyes wide with wonder.

Her grandfather smiled in return. “I’ll start our pancakes, Eva, while you think about it,” he said, humming a cheerful tune as he and Chloe headed for the kitchen.

Eva looked down at the small golden key that hung from the chain around her neck, wondering to which special lock it belonged.

Suddenly, she had an idea. “I know!” she cried happily. “I bet this is a key to Grandfather’s house. Maybe he wants me to visit him more!” But when she opened the door and held up the key, she could see it was far too small for the large lock.

“Hmmm...” Eva said, trying to think of where her shiny little key might belong. Suddenly she remembered the small lock on the side of the grandfather clock that chimed every hour.

“That must be it,” she said, turning to where the old clock stood. Grandfather knows I am learning to tell time. Maybe his clock is the present.” But when Eva tried the key in the small lock, it did not fit. This was turning out to be quite a puzzle indeed.

Then, Eva had another idea.

“Grandfather!” Eva called out happily, certain she had solved the puzzle. “May I go into your office, please?”

“You may, Eva,” her grandfather called from the kitchen, where she could hear him mixing batter in a bowl.

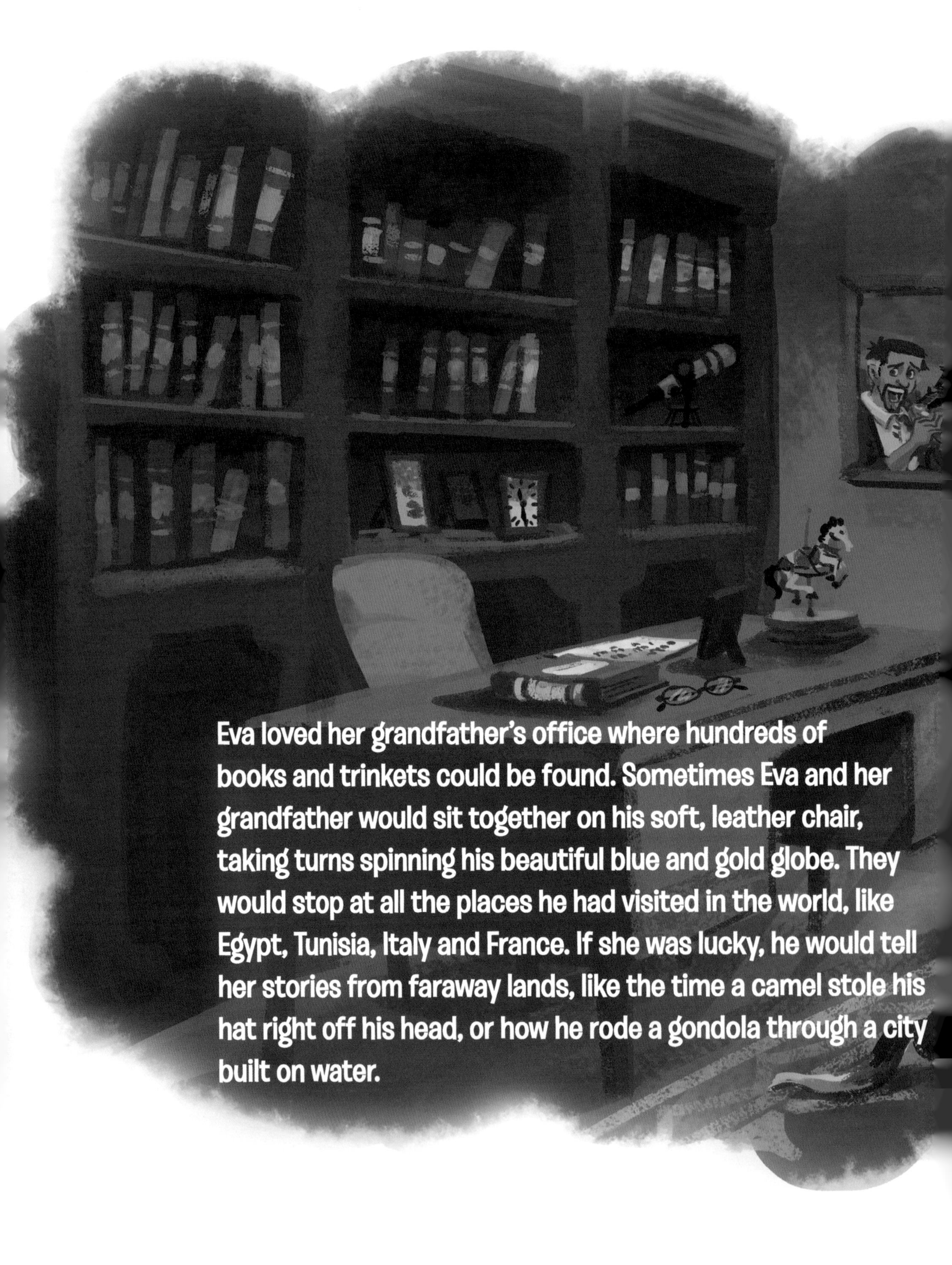

Eva loved her grandfather's office where hundreds of books and trinkets could be found. Sometimes Eva and her grandfather would sit together on his soft, leather chair, taking turns spinning his beautiful blue and gold globe. They would stop at all the places he had visited in the world, like Egypt, Tunisia, Italy and France. If she was lucky, he would tell her stories from faraway lands, like the time a camel stole his hat right off his head, or how he rode a gondola through a city built on water.

The farthest Eva had traveled from home was to San Diego to see the polar bears at the zoo, and while it had been a wonderful trip, she dreamed of visiting the pyramids and watery canals her grandfather spoke of. And she especially wanted to try an éclair beside the famous Eiffel Tower.

Remembering the key once more, Eva headed for her grandfather's desk, where one of her favorite ornaments, a white horse that played a soft melody when you wound it, could be found.

"This has to be it," Eva thought happily.

She carefully lifted the horse up and, to her delight, the key fit perfectly. But it would not turn, neither left nor right. Eva sighed, feeling discouraged and out of ideas.

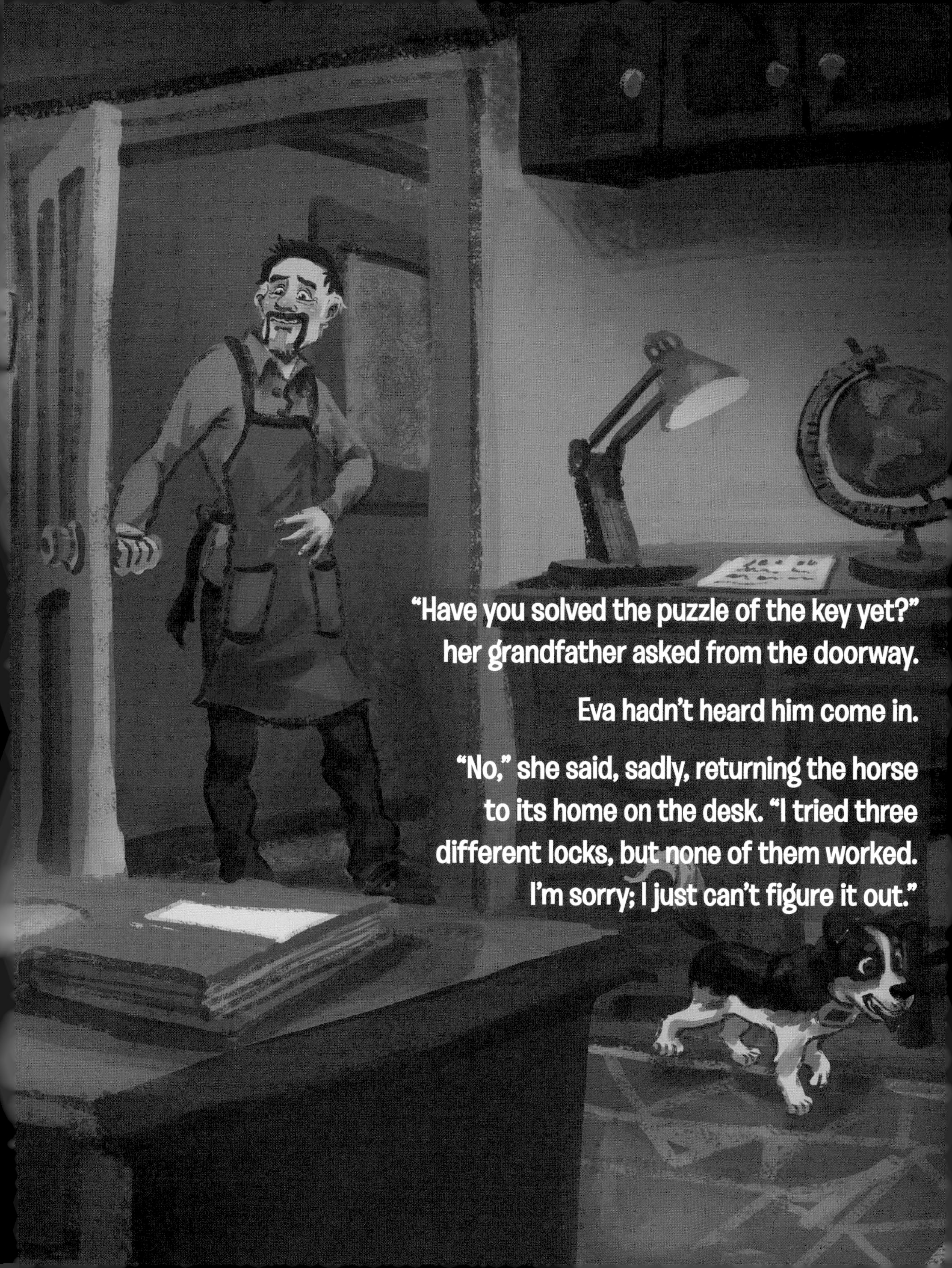

"Have you solved the puzzle of the key yet?" her grandfather asked from the doorway.

Eva hadn't heard him come in.

"No," she said, sadly, returning the horse to its home on the desk. "I tried three different locks, but none of them worked. I'm sorry; I just can't figure it out."

Her grandfather smiled warmly, wrapping her in a big hug. He smelled of flour and sweet blueberries. Placing Eva on his knee, he sat down in the familiar leather chair, while Chloe found her usual spot on the soft mat next to them.

"Not to worry, Eva," her grandfather said, brightly, so that Eva couldn't help but smile in return. "I will give you another hint."

"Thank you, Grandfather," she said, hopeful once more.

He lifted up the key so they both could see it, and then he spoke slowly. "Eva, do you know what invisible means?" he asked.

"Yes, Grandfather," Eva replied. "Invisible means that you can't see it."

"You're right, Eva," he said, proudly. "Now, can you think of some things that are invisible?" he asked.

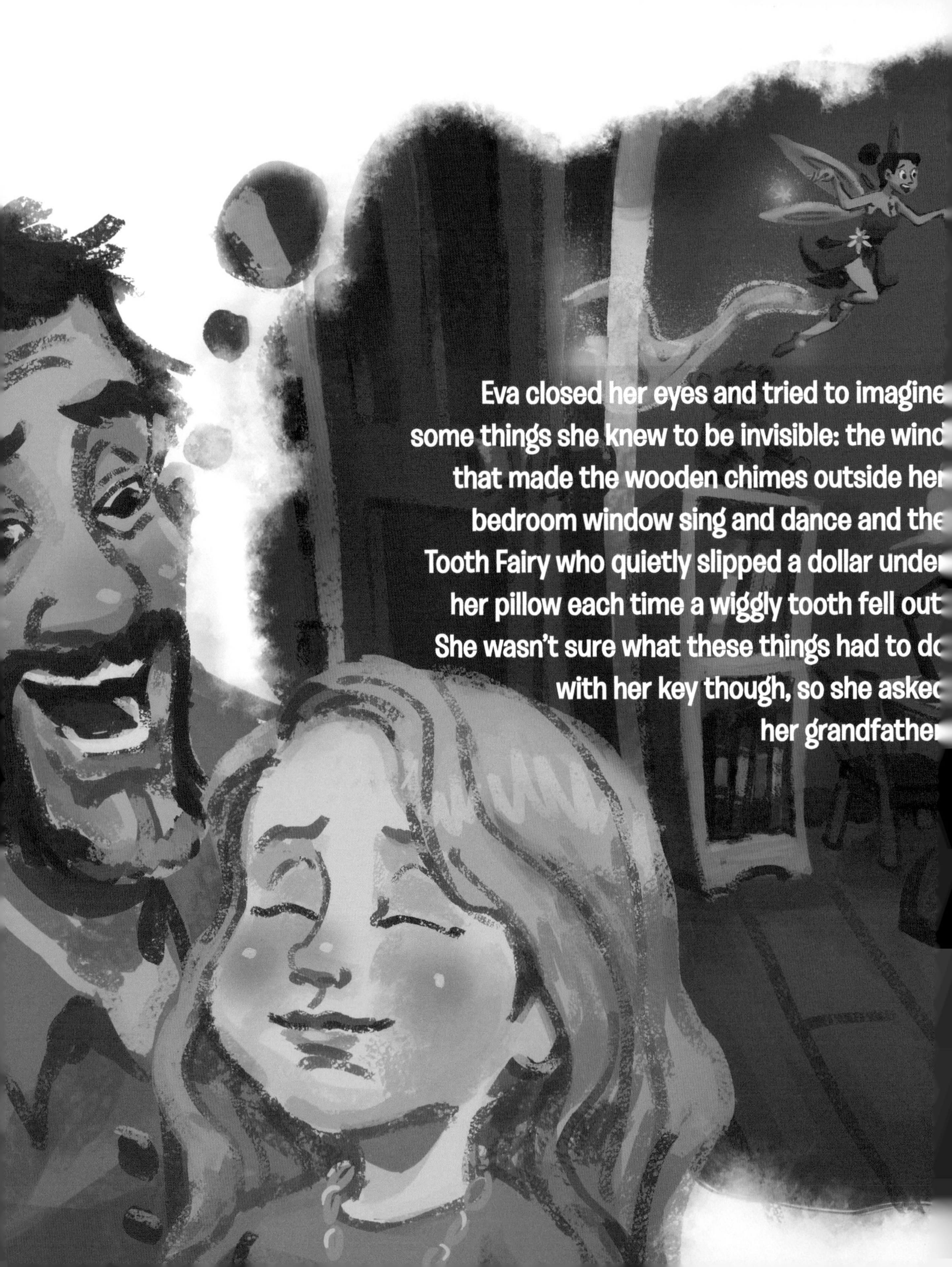

Eva closed her eyes and tried to imagine some things she knew to be invisible: the wind that made the wooden chimes outside her bedroom window sing and dance and the Tooth Fairy who quietly slipped a dollar under her pillow each time a wiggly tooth fell out. She wasn't sure what these things had to do with her key though, so she asked her grandfather.

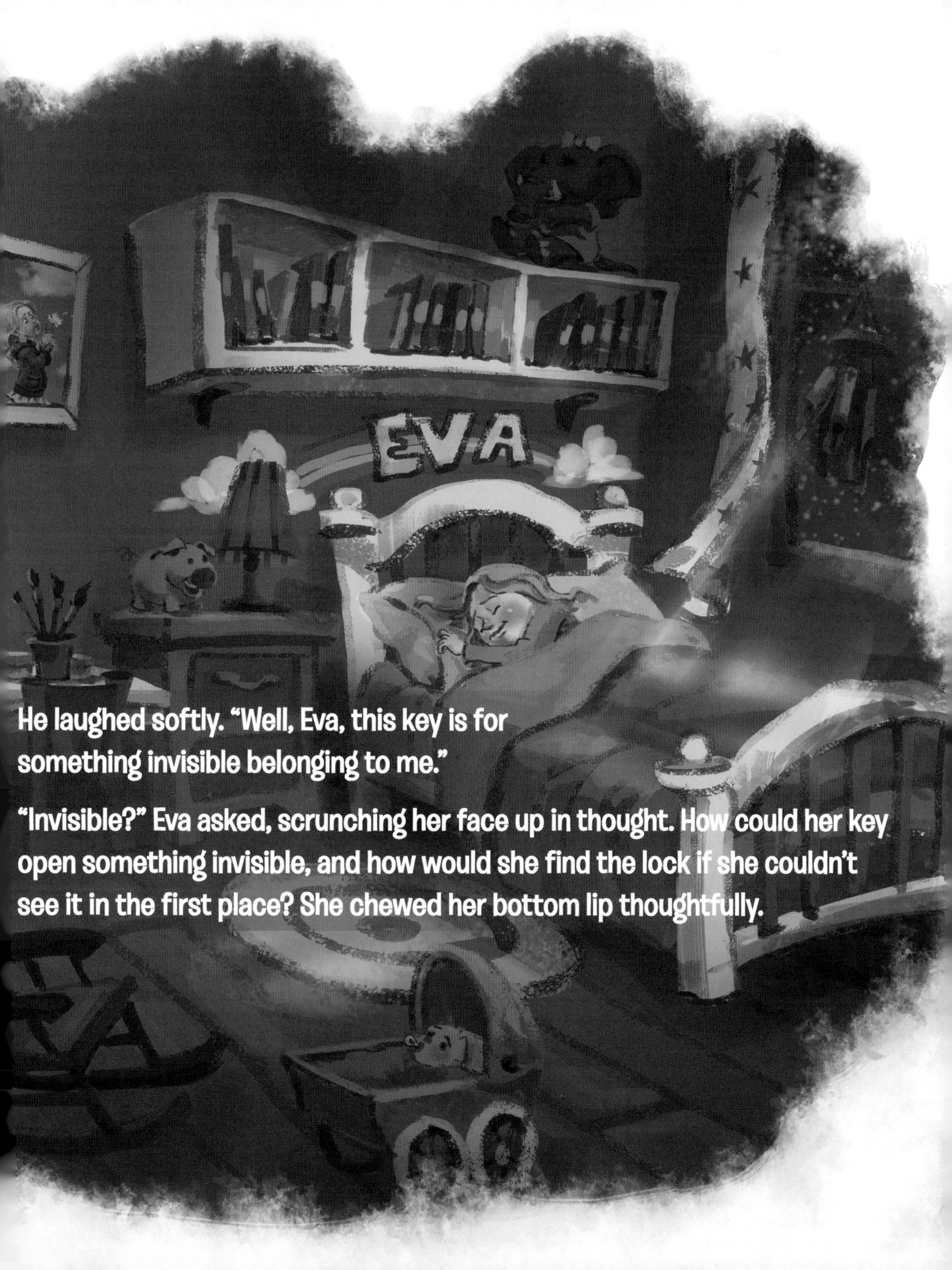

He laughed softly. "Well, Eva, this key is for something invisible belonging to me."

"Invisible?" Eva asked, scrunching her face up in thought. How could her key open something invisible, and how would she find the lock if she couldn't see it in the first place? She chewed her bottom lip thoughtfully.

"Wait!" Eva gasped. "I think I know exactly what this key is for!"

"What is it, Eva?" her grandfather asked, smiling patiently.

She placed her key on his chest, the gold shining brilliantly against his bright blue apron. "Well, Grandfather," Eva began, "you said this key is for something belonging to you."

"That's correct, Eva," he replied, nodding.

"And it's for something invisible, which means I can't see it."

"Also correct," he said.

Eva smiled joyfully as she realized the answer had been right in front of her all along. "Grandfather," she beamed, gently turning the little key against his chest, "this is the key to your heart!"

"You're right, Eva," her grandfather laughed, heartily. "You have solved the puzzle. You have the key to my heart.

Eva smiled, appreciating her key even more now that she knew what it was for.

"Now, are you ready for some very special birthday pancakes?" he asked.

"Yes!" Eva said, happily. She was starving.

Her grandfather lifted her up in the air so that she could see the tops of all the bookshelves, and then he placed her gently down next to Chloe, who sniffed the air and let out a playful whine, nuzzling her soft head against Eva's open hand.

"I think Chloe is hungry too," her grandfather laughed.

The three headed for the door, leaving the cozy office behind.

Suddenly, Eva stopped. "Grandfather," Eva began, taking his hand and placing it on her chest.

"Yes, Eva?" he asked, looking down at her.

"I just want you to know that you don't need a key to *my* heart," she said solemnly.

"Oh?" her grandfather asked.

"You've had it all along."

Her grandfather smiled, his eyes sparkling. "You are one very special seven-year-old, Eva. Now let's eat!"